D E F

J M

R T

Z

THE HULLABALOO ABC

THE HULLA

BEVERLY CLEARY

illustrated by

TED RAND

Morrow Junior Books
NEW YORK

BALOO

ABC

Watercolors were used for the full-color illustrations.
The text type is 22-point Palatino.

Published by Morrow Junior Books
a division of William Morrow and Company, Inc.
1350 Avenue of the Americas, New York, NY 10019.
www.williammorrow.com

Printed in Singapore at Tien Wah Press.

1 3 5 7 9 10 8 6 4 2

Library of Congress Cataloging-in-Publication Data
Cleary, Beverly.
The hullabaloo ABC/by Beverly Cleary; illustrated by Ted Rand.—Rev. ed.
p. cm.
Summary: An alphabet book in which three children demonstrate all the fun that is
to be had by making and hearing every kind of noise as they dash about on the farm.
ISBN 0-688-15182-5 (trade)—ISBN 0-688-15183-3 (library)
[1. Noise—Fiction.   2. Farm life—Fiction.   3. Stories in rhyme.   4. Alphabet.]
I. Rand, Ted, ill.   II. Title.   PZ8.3.C55Hu 1998   [E]—dc21   97-6457   CIP AC

To Keith and Margaret
—BC

To my grandson Luke Schaller
—TR

A a

for Aha!
I see you.

Bb

for Boo!
We see you, too.

C c

for Cock-a-doodle-doo,
The rooster's crow.
Clatter down the steps,
Come on, let's go!

Dd

for Ding-dong.
Ring this bell,
Drum on the washtub,
Yell down the well.

E e

for Echo.
"HELLO!" we shout.
"Hello!" the echo bounces out.

F f

for Flutter,
Sound of wings.
Off fly the blackbirds,
Pesky things.

G g

for Grunt.
That's the pig.
Nothing moves him.
He's too big.

Hh

for Hee-haw,
The donkey's bray.
Throw him some oats
And the horses neigh.

I i

for Inhale.
M-m-m. Sniff this rose.
Look! A bee
Buzzing by my nose!

Jj

for Jabber
From a bossy jay.
We think he's saying,
"Go 'way! Go 'way!"

K k

for Kerchoo!
What a big sneeze!
It startles the rabbit
Nibbling the peas.

L l
for Laugh.
Let's make a big racket.
There's a pail.
Grab a stick and whack it.

Mm

for Moo
From a cow in her stall.
Her calf is hungry.
Hear him bawl.

Nn

for Noises,
Clucks and cackles.
A hawk!
It scatters the hens
And makes them squawk.

O o

for Ouch!
I've stubbed my toe.
Never mind.
Get up, let's go!

Pp

for Putt-putt
From the tractor there.
Bang! It stopped.
It needs repair.

Qq

for Quack-quack.
See the ducks and the cat.
Back to the barn, kitty.
Shoo! Scat!

R r
for Rumble.
Thunder rolls, lightning rips.
Race for the barn.
Watch out! Don't trip.

S s

for Sh-h-h.
A squeak in the hay?
It's a mouse
Scuttling away.

Tt

for Toot-toot.
Wave to the train
Clickity-clacking
Through the rain.

U u

for Ugh.
Slick, wet mud.
Run, skid,
Thump, thud.

Vv

for Voice.
Did someone call?
Quick! Up on the horse.
Try not to fall.

Ww

for Whoop.
Giddy-up, let's go!
Wait. The horse whinnies.
Whoa! Whoa!

X x

for Exclaim,
"Enough! We're through!"
Father is shouting
And Mother, too.

Yy

for Yodel
With all our might.
Now they know
That we're all right.

Z z

for Zoom.
See us run.
Hear our noise,
Watch our fun!

A B C

G H I

N O P Q

U V W